on the Run

Random House Australia Pty Ltd
20 Alfred Street, Milsons Point NSW 2061
http://www.randomhouse.com.au

Sydney New York Toronto
London Auckland Johannesburg
and agencies throughout the world.

First published in 2001
Text copyright © Phil Cummings

National Library of Australia Cataloguing-in-Publication Data

Cummings, Phil, 1957– .
On the run

ISBN 1 74051 701 6.

1. Suspense fiction. I. Title.

A823.3

Cover photograph by Reece Scannell.
Cover design by Gayna Murphy: Greendot Design.
Author photograph by Sue Cummings.
Typeset by Asset Typesetting Pty Ltd in 13.5/22 Gill Sans.
Printed by Griffin Press.

on R the un

ANOTHER RENTED HOUSE MYSTERY

PHIL CUMMINGS

RANDOM HOUSE AUSTRALIA

*To the Ravlich family
and the memories of the
first handwritten scrawls.*

Chapter 1

It was a hot, humid day. Barry Carter looked up at the sky. Huge, dark clouds on the horizon were creeping slowly toward him. They lit up occasionally with flashes of sheet lightning and then rumbled like a giant with a bellyache. A bead of sweat ran from his forehead down between his eyes and along the length of his nose, where it reached the very tip. It hung there until he lifted his hand and wiped it away.

There came another roll of thunder, louder this time. Barry didn't like thunder and lightning. He'd been scared of it since he was two years old. He couldn't remember much from back then but the one thing he could remember was how thunder and lightning had interfered with his toilet training schedule. For a toddler trying to break the nappy habit he was doing pretty well, and was wearing pants without nappies for most of the day. But then, a big storm came. It was night time and Barry was sitting on the toilet. There was a great flash of lightning and clap of thunder. The lights went out and Barry was trapped in the dark in the toilet, alone. The toilet started bubbling and gurgling just at that moment, and he was sure there was something horrible lurking in the depths below that was going to swallow him. Barry screamed. Harley, his big black dog, who wasn't much older than Barry, came wandering in to see what all the fuss was about. Barry didn't know it was Harley. In the darkness he thought Harley was some great hairy beast. Barry had tried to stand on the toilet to get away from the beast, but fell off. When his mum came in with her torch she found Barry flat on his back on the floor, kicking and screaming as Harley tried to lick away his tears. For some time after that on little Barry's night-time visits to the toilet he would carry his father's torch in one hand and a giant inflatable baseball bat in the other.

Barry was remembering that night as he stared nervously up at the sky. It was getting darker. The lightning was closer, the flashes brighter. The thunder was increasing in volume. Barry suddenly felt as though he needed to go to the toilet, but he strongly resisted the urge. A nervous shiver ran down his back. He rolled his shoulders to try to make it go away.

Suddenly, someone grabbed his arm. He jumped. 'Huh!'

Sarah frowned at him. 'Are you all right, Barry?'

Looking jittery, Barry was quick to respond.

'Me? Yeah, I'm fine,' he said, rocking awkwardly from side to side. 'Why wouldn't I be? I'm not scared of anything.'

Sarah tilted her head to one side. 'No one said you were.'

'Right then,' Barry nodded firmly. 'Good.'

Jack chuckled. 'Barry, hurry up and hammer the seats on will you, before the rain comes.'

Barry looked around at his friends and neighbours. There were four of them. Andy and his twin sister Megan, Jack from across the road and Sarah from the corner. They were all squatting there in Sarah's front yard surrounded by hammers, nails, old seats and an old door on wheels that Barry had once used unsuccessfully as a giant skateboard. They had all thought making the giant skateboard was a great idea. That was until Barry's big accident. He had gone flying down Ridley Road completely out of control and nearly got himself run over by

Dennis, the young guy who was living at number twenty-two, the rented house. They all liked Dennis, after they got to know him, and he was now in Hollywood making films. The rented house was empty again, waiting for a new tenant.

The disaster of Barry's crash on the giant skateboard had not dampened their spirits for very long. Sarah had another plan for the old door on wheels. Her father was a builder and had been working at a demolition site. He was helping pull down an old church and had brought home some wooden seats. Sarah thought it would be cool to attach them to the old door and make a go-cart, but not just for one person — for four or five people. Sort of a go-cart bus. The others had thought it a fantastic idea and they were all helping to make the necessary modifications.

Barry had taken charge of the hammer and

was helping an unsure Jack to hammer in the very long nails. The twins were holding the seats steady while Barry hammered.

Jack was handing Barry the nails. He looked at Barry's earring, a silver motorbike. 'You know Barry,' he said thoughtfully, 'that earring is a concern to me and it should be to you as well.'

Barry rolled his eyes in Jack's direction. 'Why?'

'Lightning.'

'Huh?'

'Lightning could strike that earring, you know. You could have your brain fried if lightning hit that.'

Barry felt his stomach churn. He didn't like the sound of this. His round face moulded itself into a look that was a mixture of fear and repulsion.

Jack continued. 'Do you know, there was once a boy ...'

Barry quickly raised two hands to stop Jack.

'Hold it right there, Jack. I don't want one of your stupid stories.'

'It's not stupid, it's very scientific.' Jack was always telling scientific stories. His mother and father both worked for a submarine corporation and that's what Jack wanted to do when he grew up. Barry didn't think much of submarines. Travelling about in a giant metal sausage, all dark and confining, didn't appeal to him at all.

Barry quickly took his earring off. He put it in his pocket. 'Right Jack, no more stories, let's just hammer these seats on before the rain comes. We want to try this out in a minute.'

He picked up the hammer and spun it skilfully in his hand. 'Right, hold the nail.'

Jack shook his head. 'I don't think so, Barry. You hold your own nail.'

Barry sighed heavily. 'I'm not going to hit your hand for goodness sake. Don't you trust me?' He puffed out his chest and tapped it with his left hand. 'This is Barry Carter you're working with here. The best hammer hand in the business.'

Jack shook his head and dropped the nail in front of Barry. 'No way, Barry. Hold it yourself.'

Barry pursed his lips. 'I *never* miss, never.'

As soon as Barry uttered those words it was obvious what was going to happen next. Harley, who was sitting on the door looking on, whined softly and turned away. The scream Barry let out when he hit his thumb was far louder than any rumble of thunder had been. He then proceeded to do a crazy dance. The sound of thunder rolled around the children while Barry spun, jumped, hopped and skipped with his thumb pushed tightly under his armpit. He spat out angry words through clenched teeth as the lightning flashed above. The pain in his thumb made him forget all about his fear. Then the rain came. It was heavy, hard rain. Huge droplets exploded on the hot road. The children ran to Sarah's verandah for cover.

Sarah shook the rain from her hair. 'Hey, great rain dance, Barry,' she quipped, patting Barry on the back. The others laughed.

Barry didn't, he was busily sucking his thumb.

Andy lifted the bottom of his T-shirt and wiped his face with it. 'What do we do now?'

'Yes, what do we do now?' echoed Megan. They often repeated things one after the other, they said it was a twin thing.

The five of them stood looking out through a heavy curtain of rain from the overflowing gutter. With the coming of the rain the lightning had faded and the thunder had softened. Barry was feeling calmer now, despite the pain in his throbbing thumb. 'The rain won't last long,' he said, looking knowledgeably up at the sky.

At that very moment it got heavier.

Sarah put her hand under the waterfall of rain from the gutter. Water splashed from her outstretched hand into the faces of her friends.

She laughed until the others retaliated. Andy whipped his hand through the thick water curtain. Jack stood back well out of the way as Megan and Barry started flinging both arms through the water in a splashing war. There was laughing, screaming, shouting and soon there were five very wet friends under Sarah's verandah.

It was as Jack was jumping back to avoid being splashed that he slipped on a large piece of black plastic covering a stack of old window frames on the verandah behind him. As if on a water slide, he slid right off the verandah out into the rain and landed with a splat on the gravel driveway. The others pointed and doubled over with laughter.

'Good idea!' Sarah shouted. 'Grab the plastic, let's make our own water slide!'

Barry put his hand up as if he were at school and jumped in front of Sarah. 'I'll go first!' he said.

They pulled at the plastic and unfolded it. It was much bigger than they had anticipated.

'Let's put it in the driveway,' said Megan.

'Good idea,' said Andy, patting her on the back.

Sarah's driveway sloped gently toward the street, perfect for water sliding. The rain had softened the driveway as well and the black plastic was very thick. They were soon all out in the rain spreading the plastic. Jack took control of securing the corners of the plastic with weights — bricks, pieces of wood, the old wooden chairs that were to be part of the go-cart bus. The plastic reached just beyond the gates at the end of the driveway and out onto the footpath. Once the plastic was ready they all ran back to the verandah — all except Barry, who was preparing himself for the first slide.

Barry stood out in the rain a few metres back from the end of the plastic. He wanted to get a decent run-up. Being the first one to test the slide wasn't enough, he was also going to have to be the best. He was the one who would show the others the way. He was a leader, an innovator, a history maker. He would always be remembered as the first to take the Great Black Plastic Water Slide. Just as he was the first to ride the giant skateboard down Ridley Road. His success was crucial.

With water dripping from his hair and eyebrows into his eyes he bent forward in his get-ready-to-run position. The others were calling to him from the verandah, like a crowd in a grandstand at an Olympic final. Barry looked over to them. 'Here goes!' he cried, giving them the thumbs up.

Megan looked at her twin brother. 'Do you think he knows what he's doing, Andy?'

Andy shrugged his shoulders. He turned to Jack. 'Do you think he knows what he's doing, Jack?'

Jack too shrugged his shoulders. He turned to Sarah. 'Hey Sarah, do you think he knows what he's doing?'

Sarah pulled her long hair into a ponytail. She tilted her head to one side and squeezed out some water. 'Of course. He would've been on one of those slip-n-slide things you can buy from the shops, wouldn't he?' She paused. Three faces were looking inquiringly at her. 'What can happen to him anyway? He'll just slide to an awkward stop if he loses it. The thing might not even work. The plastic might not be slippery enough to get up a good speed.'

Jack rubbed his chin. 'Maybe I'll just tell him to take it easy on the first go.'

'Good idea,' the others agreed in chorus.

The rain suddenly became heavier. The sound of the downpour on the roof of the verandah was deafening.

Barry smiled in anticipation. Perfect. The

more water the better. The plastic would be really slippery now.

Jack called to Barry. 'Barry! Barry! Don't run too fast on the first go.'

Squinting, and trying to brush the rain from his face, Barry heard only parts of Jack's message. 'Yeah, I'll go fast on the first go, don't worry about that, Jack.'

Jack shook his head. 'No! Slow.'

'No, okay. I won't go slow.'

The others waved their arms to try to get their message across.

Barry looked at them and waved back. They're wishing me luck, he thought. What great friends I've got.

Meanwhile, Harley had sat himself under the old chairs stacked at the other end of the verandah and turned his head away. He couldn't watch. He closed his eyes and pretended he was asleep. He heard Barry begin his journey.

'Yahoo!' Barry shouted. He pumped his chubby legs as hard as he could as he ran toward the plastic. He'd seen these sorts of things advertised on television. Long bits of coloured plastic sprayed with water. The kids in the ads had slipped along on their bellies, arms outstretched in front of them. Barry would go faster than them.

His pounding feet sloshed on the muddy driveway as he gathered speed. His damp face was a picture of determination. The crowd stood up in the grandstand as he approached the plastic and prepared himself for the dive.

Barry concentrated. His attention was keenly focused. The dive was very important. He was at full speed now and the plastic was looming. As he took the last few paces before the dive his face stretched with anticipation. Then, with a deep breath followed by a loud cry of excitement, he thrust his arms to the air and flung himself full length at the plastic.

'*Yeehagghh!*' he shouted. He hit the plastic stomach first with a loud *oomph!* Barry was away, sliding at great speed like a big cake of soap dropped into a slippery bathtub.

He couldn't believe how fast he was going. Water splashed into his face as he hit the puddles that had formed on the uneven plastic. He was halfway down the plastic now and the street was looming ever closer. The concrete footpath, the kerb, the hard bitumen. He flew over a small bump in the driveway and became airborne for a split second.

It was at that moment he realised he was out of control.

Chapter 2

Barry was slipping about on the wet plastic in obvious panic. His outstretched arms were pushing furiously against the plastic in a feeble attempt to slow himself down. Water rose in thin fans from his hands and hit him in the face, making it almost impossible to see what lay ahead. As his speeding body continued to cut through the water Barry did everything he could to try to gain control. His legs were kicking about like a frog in a fit. He even tried pushing his forehead into the plastic to see if that would slow him down. He knew the road wasn't far off. He had to stop before he skidded out onto it.

The spectators on the verandah were excited at first. 'Wow! Look at him go!' Megan cried.

'Just look at him go,' echoed Andy.

There was even applause for the first few metres, until they saw Barry flapping about in a panic. They too could see the dangers ahead.

Jack moved closer to the edge of the verandah. 'He can't stop. I knew he should've taken it easy.'

'Well, we did try to tell him,' nodded Sarah.

'Maybe we should try to stop him,' said Jack, taking a step out from under cover into the rain.

'It's too late for that,' said Sarah quickly. 'But we'd better be there to pick him up.' With that they jumped from the verandah and ran toward the street.

Barry was still on his belly but he was spinning now. Spinning and shouting. 'Whoa! I can't stop.'

Around he went. 'Help meeeee!' The more he tried to slow down the more he spun. One second he was heading toward the street feet first, then the next he spun around and was sliding head-first toward disaster. Sliding from the plastic feet first was the better option, but he had no control over that.

The heavy rain and Barry's ear-piercing cries blocked out the sound of a vehicle revving its way up Ridley Road toward Sarah's house. It wasn't a car. It was an old van, riddled with rusty dents and scratches. The windscreen wipers were slow and ineffective. The brakes probably were as well.

Resigned to skidding onto the hard surface of the footpath, Barry gritted his teeth as he sped toward the end of the plastic. His friends were running down the driveway after him, pushing through the veil of rain.

Sarah was the first to see the van. Its engine

was rattling as it approached them. The headlights glowed a dull yellow. The driver's face was pressed close to the windscreen. Sarah cupped her hands to her mouth and shouted to Barry. 'Look out for the van!'

Her cry brought the van to the attention of her friends. 'Barry! Look out for the van!' They hollered, pointing.

Their cries were of no use to Barry. He couldn't hear them properly and even if he could there was nothing he could do. He hit the footpath side on and rolled like a log down a slope toward the road.

The driver of the van didn't see him. Harley was watching Barry from the edge of the verandah. He lifted his snout to the sky and howled mournfully. 'Hoooowwwwlll.'

Barry was tumbling across the footpath. The van was gaining speed, its tyres splashing through the rain on the wet road. There seemed no possible way to avoid a terrible accident. It seemed Barry was doomed.

But then, no one had counted on the recently excavated trench that ran along the side of the road. The trench had been the subject of angry discussions between Sarah's father and the telephone company for the past two days because he had been unable to park his truck in the driveway to load and unload. The coloured flags that had hung along its length as a warning had fallen into the mud. Out of sight, out of mind. The trench wasn't quite a metre wide but it was very deep.

Just when it looked as though Barry was going to roll under the wheels of the passing van, he disappeared completely. The van moved on down the road, the driver didn't even notice Barry rolling into the trench.

Megan put her hands to her cheeks in shock. 'Where did he go?' she cried.

'He's in the trench,' Sarah answered as she ran to Barry's aid. The others were quick to follow. They stood at the edge of the trench and gazed down at Barry. He was flat on his back and partly submerged in mud. His ears weren't visible, nor were his hands. He was making a high-pitched groaning sound.

Harley arrived on the scene and peered into the hole. He wagged his tail and barked when he saw his master.

Barry sat up slowly and then struggled to his feet. No one volunteered to jump in and help him. Harley slapped Barry's face with his tongue just as soon as Barry stood and looked out from the trench. Barry pushed him away.

'Are you okay?' asked Jack, offering Barry a helping hand.

Megan reached down and offered to help as well.

Barry was frowning. He looked grumpily

around to each of his friends. They all felt guilty although they had no reason to.

Sarah felt the need to defend herself. 'You can't blame us, you wanted to be first. We told you to slow down.' She looked to the others. 'Didn't we, gang?'

Three heads nodded furiously in agreement with Sarah's statement.

Mumbling to himself, Barry scrambled clumsily from the trench. He was a mess. He shook himself and so did Harley. He looked back into the trench. 'That could've been my grave, you know.' He turned to Sarah. 'You could've reminded me it was there.'

Sarah raised her eyebrows. 'You were very lucky it *was* there!' she said forcefully. 'If it wasn't for that trench the van would've got you.'

Barry looked puzzled. 'What van?' he asked.

No sooner had he asked the question than there was loud *bang* from the bottom of Ridley

Road. It startled Barry. He jumped, lost his footing in the mud and fell back into the trench.

The others ignored Barry. Their attention was immediately drawn toward the van. A cloud of thick blue smoke rose from the back of it.

Barry complained as he scrambled to his feet. 'Thanks a heap, you guys. Leave a guy to die why don't you.'

He crawled from the trench and followed their interested gaze. The van was parked at the front of number twenty-two, the rented house, and smoke was still coming from its tailpipe.

'Do you think it's on fire?' said Andy, frowning.

'Looks like it,' said Megan.

'Maybe they need help,' said Jack.

Sarah was thoughtful. 'Should I go inside and call the fire brigade?'

Barry tried to wipe some of the mud from his face but all he succeeded in doing was adding muddy lines. 'Don't be silly, the thing's just backfired, that's all. The smoke will settle in a minute.'

They all waited.

There was a brief pause before Jack said, 'Who was in that van anyway?' He looked at each of his friends in turn. 'Did anyone notice?' They all shook their heads.

'It was too wet to see properly,' said Sarah. 'Whoever it was had their face close to the windscreen but because the wipers weren't working properly I couldn't make anything out.'

The smoke was finally settling. Barry took a couple of steps forward. He moved slowly, awkwardly, like a big swamp creature. 'Hang on, the van door's opening.' He turned back to the others. 'Looks like we have a new neighbour.' He smiled. 'Let's go meet them, we must let them know that this is a friendly neighbourhood.' Barry had his best friendly face on. It was so sweet it was sickening.

'Oh come off it, Barry Carter,' Sarah scoffed. 'You just want to be nosy.'

Barry put his hands on his hips. He opened his mouth to defend himself but couldn't think of what to say.

'Besides,' laughed Andy. 'I don't think you'd make a very good impression, Barry.' There were laughs all round.

The muddy swamp creature moved threateningly toward Andy.

'I don't think any of us would,' said Jack quickly. 'We all look like drowned rats.'

There was laughter as they all realised what they must look like.

'We can wait though, and see who gets out of the van,' said Sarah.

There was another loud bang and a puff of smoke from the van. The engine was turned off. The driver got out. The children couldn't see for the smoke. They could make out a figure but the smoke and the rain made it very difficult to see more.

The young, friendly neighbours hastily repositioned themselves around the trench, each striving for a clearer view. The newcomer made things worse by running from the van to the house. There was a long dark coat and an enormous umbrella. Straining their eyes to see, the friends moved in the direction of the rented house, but to no avail. No one saw anything that would give them an indication of who or what the person was. It was guessing time.

'What do you reckon?' said Barry. 'Male or female?'

'Hmm, hard to tell,' said Jack, tapping his chin thoughtfully. 'But I think from the way it ran that it's a female.'

Megan agreed. 'Yes, female, definitely.'

Andy nodded. 'Definitely.'

Sarah was unusually quiet. Barry waddled over to her. 'What do you think, Sarah?'

Sarah narrowed her eyes. 'I have to disagree. I think it was a male.'

Megan looked at Barry. 'What about you? What do you think?'

Barry was the only one who hadn't offered an opinion. He could feel the others looking at him, waiting for his response. He felt a kind of power over them. He milked the moment for all it was worth, bowing his head, rubbing his forehead, frowning thoughtfully. He took a deep breath and looked down his nose at his friends. He was now behaving like the professor of swamp creatures.

'Now, I think, taking everything into account ... the running, the way the arms moved, the somewhat unusual rounded shoulders ...' He paused again, putting his hands behind his back. 'My friends, I think our new neighbour is ... is a

…' He leant forward for the final delivery of his judgment. 'A gorilla!'

He laughed raucously at his own joke. He walked about tossing his head back and slapping his knees, laughing. No one else was laughing. They screwed up their faces.

'You're the gorilla, Barry,' said Sarah, bumping playfully into him. The others followed suit and Barry was laughing so hard that he could do little to retaliate. They bumped him around in circles, which wasn't a very good idea really. Barry found himself getting dizzy. He tried to stop laughing and keep himself steady but he couldn't. He wobbled away from his friends and still laughing, slipped and fell once more into the trench. '*Agghhhhhh!*'

Chapter 3

The following day was bright and sunny. A few fluffy clouds were drifting across an otherwise clear blue sky. Barry was sleeping in and having a wonderful dream about driving a red Ferrari. He was cruising into the schoolyard to show his friends when a loud explosion shattered his dream. He sat upright. *Bang!* There was another one. He jumped out of bed quicker than he had ever done before, put on a T-shirt (inside out) pulled on his tracksuit pants (back to front), stepped into a sneaker and one black boot and ran from the house to see what was happening.

His hair was sticking up in spikes, twisted in bumpy swirls, sitting in little ridges. He didn't give it a thought. *Bang!* Another explosion. They were coming from the street. He ran through the house, out the front door and up the driveway. He stood on the footpath and looked down Ridley Road.

The first thing he noticed was a large cloud of blue smoke drifting into the sky from the bottom of Ridley Road. The van at number twenty-two had started up. Barry was rubbing his eyes when he heard Jack call out to him from across the street. 'Get dressed in a hurry, Barry?'

Barry was puzzled until he looked down at his shirt, his pants and then his shoes. Jack was laughing and he wasn't the only one. All of Barry's friends had rushed from their houses at the sound of the explosions. They were standing next to Jack. Laughing, they all waved to Barry. Barry smiled a crooked smile, blushed, then moved slowly toward his letterbox and stood behind the big bush there. He took his T-shirt off and put it on properly. He wasn't game to do the same with his pants, so he left them. He couldn't do anything about his shoes, he didn't want to go inside in case he missed something. If the van blew up he wanted to be there to see it.

The van began moving. It turned, backfired again and smoked its way slowly up Ridley Road. Perfect, they'd all get a good look at their new neighbour now. The van crawled towards them, jerking awkwardly. It coughed and spluttered. Blue smoke rose in puffy clouds.

The small crowd of observers craned their necks and strained their eyes. They all looked at the driver, an old woman with very long grey hair that hung like two thick curtains at either side of her face. It was hard to see in through the windscreen but she wore thick glasses and her face was wrinkly, they could see that much. The children waved. She was hunched over the steering wheel of the van and didn't turn her head to acknowledge them. Sarah called out to her. And so did Jack. 'Hello. Hello!' But she didn't respond. She saw them, though. She must have.

As soon as the van passed, the children ran onto the street and stood in the cloud of smoke it left behind. They silently watched the van turn slowly out of Ridley Road.

'Right,' said Andy. 'I think it was a female.'

'She ran pretty fast yesterday for an old woman, didn't she?' said Barry.

'Yes, she did actually,' Sarah agreed.

'She's probably a fit old woman,' said Megan.

'Maybe,' said Jack. 'But let's not stand here thinking about it. Let's go to the meeting bush.' They all headed for Barry's house. The huge bush near his letterbox was a perfect hide.

Harley arrived just as the children were

running through the gate. He greeted them with the usual furious tail-wagging and friendly woof. They responded with a ruffle of his ears or a scratch of his chest. He was happy. They were *his* friends as well as Barry's.

'She looked horrible,' said Megan, who was first to arrive. 'Maybe she's sick.'

'I agree, she looked awful,' said Andy, following her closely.

Megan looked up at Barry's hair. She had to say *something*. 'Have a bad night, Barry?' she asked with genuine concern. 'Nightmares can really toss you about in bed, can't they?'

Barry put his hands to his head and tried to flatten his hair down. 'No, I'm fine.'

Sarah smiled. 'Give up, Barry.'

They all shuffled themselves into a tight huddle under the bush. 'So we have an old woman living in the rented house now,' said Andy, stating the obvious. 'Bit of a change from Dennis.'

'Her hair was really long, wasn't it?' said Sarah. 'Quite strange for someone as old as her.'

'Not really,' said Megan. 'Our grandma's got long hair. Hasn't she, Andy?'

'She has.' Andy nodded. 'But she wears it in a neat ponytail, not all straggly.'

'Oh well,' said Jack suddenly. 'Now that we've sorted that out there's no point hanging about here.'

Barry could sense the disappointment in the group, especially after the day had started with such a bang. It was all fizzing out to nothing. Barry had to do something.

He leant forward, pushing his face into the huddle. His eyes narrowed and rolled shiftily. 'Do you know what I think?' he said in a low, gruff tone. 'I think she looks like a witch.' There was laughter.

Jack slapped Barry's back. 'Oh come on, Barry. That has got to be one of the silliest things I have ever heard you say. Or is this another one of your jokes like the gorilla joke?'

Sarah shook her head as she tried to control her giggling.

Barry was speechless for a few seconds. He was serious. 'Laugh if you like,' he said, raising his eyebrows, 'but I don't like the look of her, witch or not.'

'Look,' said Sarah calmly. 'The poor woman has probably just moved here to get some peace and quiet. Let's just leave it. We'll get to know her soon enough.'

'If she wants peace and quiet,' said Barry, lifting himself to his feet, 'she should get rid of that van. She can't let it backfire like that every time she starts it up, especially in the mornings. And *extra* especially on weekends.'

Everyone was suddenly quiet. They were lost for words, unsure of what to say next. Barry stood up and stretched. The others found themselves staring at his mismatched shoes.

He knew what they were looking at so he wandered from the huddle, yawning. 'I'm going to have my breakfast, I'll see you later.'

The group broke up.

'I wish Dennis still lived there,' said Megan. 'He was more fun than some old woman.'

Andy nodded. 'Mmm, he was.'

An hour or so later Barry came flying out of his driveway on his bike with Harley bounding along in hot pursuit. He saw Jack sitting in his front yard under a tree, doing something scientific with batteries, wires, a motor, wheels and a small propeller. Barry rode into Jack's yard at full speed. He headed straight for Jack who was concentrating so deeply he didn't see Barry flying toward him. Barry pedalled until he was close enough, then he put the brakes on hard and sent the back wheel of his bike skidding through Jack's experiment.

Startled, Jack cried out in shock and tumbled backwards. As soon as he was able, he sprung to his feet. He was furious. He looked down at his scattered bits and pieces. 'Barry!' he hollered, pointing to the ground. 'Look what you've done!'

Barry looked to where Jack was pointing. He didn't see the batteries, wires and other things, he was only interested in his skid mark on the lawn. 'Yeah, it's not bad but I can do a bigger one,' he said.

Jack ground his teeth and angrily mumbled something under his breath. He fell to his knees and began collecting his bits and pieces. Harley was sitting on the propeller wagging his tail. Jack pushed him away and pulled the propeller from beneath him. Harley stuck his big tongue in Jack's left ear. Wiping his ear, Jack said, 'If you have damaged any of this stuff, so help me Barry, I'll …'

Barry took no notice of Jack's anger. He knew he didn't mean it.

'What do you want anyway, Barry?' said Jack without looking up.

'I've got news.'

'What news?'

'News about the rented house.'

'About the gorilla or the witch?' said Jack sarcastically.

'You can make fun of me if you like but you wait till I tell you what I've found out.'

Jack stopped and looked up at Barry. He knew that if he didn't show an interest Barry would never go away. He sighed. 'Okay, what is it, Barry? Has she changed you into a frog, or Harley into a newt?'

Barry turned his head to one side and slid a curious glance Jack's way. 'A what?'

'A newt.'

Barry's face was blank. Jack sighed again. 'Oh never mind. Just tell me your news.'

Barry turned his bike away from Jack. 'In a minute. I'll go and get the others first. We'll meet in the bush at my place.' He started to ride away.

'Just tell me, Barry,' Jack called. 'I don't want to come to a meeting, I want to finish this.'

Barry rode on. 'I'll see you in the bush,' he called back.

Jack stood and watched Barry ride away. He thought about not turning up for the meeting. He could just ignore Barry. But then again, Barry sounded pretty excited and he didn't want to miss out on anything.

And so the children gathered in Barry's letterbox-bush. Harley sat in the middle of the circle. It was the best place for him. Ten hands rubbing, patting and scratching was heaven. Harley loved the bush meetings. He lay on his back, legs in the air and moaned contentedly as his belly was rubbed all over.

The friends leant forward in anticipation as Barry prepared to deliver his news. 'Last night my dad came home late, about ten thirty. He had been out and bought another Ferrari seat.'

'That's good, Barry,' said Andy with keen interest. 'He's got two now, hasn't he?' He thought Barry's dad's idea of collecting bits of a Ferrari until he got a complete one was great. Barry had promised Andy a ride in it when the time came.

Barry was sidetracked by Andy's comment. 'Yeah, he's got the driver's seat and the passenger's seat. We can sit in them and watch telly together. Sometimes Dad likes to fool around and pretend we're going for a drive. He makes the engine noise and everything.'

'Barry, get on with it, will you,' Sarah interrupted, trying not to imagine Barry's dad making car noises. He was a big man with a beard, shaved head and tattoos on his arms.

Barry continued. 'Right, sorry. Well, Dad was lifting the seat out of the four-wheel drive when he saw the van go past. He was talking to Mum about it just a few minutes ago. He said it was crawling along very slowly, he didn't think it was going to make it down to number twenty-two. He called out to the *young* girl driving it and asked if she needed a push. She said no but he said she looked young, just out of school. Those were his very words. *Young, just out of school.* That woman we saw wasn't young and just out of school.'

Barry stopped. Everyone waited for him to continue with the story, to say something else, but he didn't.

Jack's shoulders slumped. 'Is that it! Is that your earth-shattering news?'

Barry glared at him. 'Well, how can she suddenly be young?'

Sarah folded her arms. 'Barry, it's probably just her daughter. People who are as old as the woman we saw might just have sons and daughters. Even grandsons and daughters.'

Barry's face went blank. He hadn't thought of that. He had thought only of witches and spells and the secret to eternal youth.

Jack stood up. 'Why must you always make a big mystery out of everything, Barry?' He walked away, mumbling.

Sarah followed and the twins weren't far behind. 'Let's go put the seats on the door at Sarah's house,' they suggested. Everyone agreed.

Barry didn't, he stayed under the bush. 'I'm not going,' he mumbled sulkily to himself. He rubbed Harley's belly. 'They'll thank me one day, mate,' he whispered. 'There's something going on down there and they will thank me for being so alert.'

He watched them walking away, chatting about what they were going to do with the go-cart bus. He became fidgety. He couldn't hear what they were saying. He couldn't stand it. 'Come on, Harley. We'd better go with them, they'll need our help.'

He ran from the bush with Harley following. 'Hey guys, wait for us.'

The others turned to see Barry bounding toward them. Sarah noticed his pants.

'Hey, Barry,' she called, smiling. 'That witch must've cast a spell on you. Your pants and shoes look a lot better than they did this morning.' There was laughter.

Barry blushed as a fluffy cloud drifted across the sun and a shadow fell over Ridley Road.

Chapter 4

It was Friday again. A whole week of school had passed and nothing at all interesting had happened in Ridley Road. There had been the occasional bang when the van at number twenty-two had started up, but nothing more. The van had hardly been there and the house seemed to be empty most of the time. In any case, the school weeks were so busy there wasn't time to do much else except go to school, do homework and go to sleep.

Barry had had a bit of excitement during the week. His father came home with a Ferrari steering wheel and gearstick. They had some fun together in the lounge room that night. Sarah too had something exciting happen; she had a new kitten. It was pure white and she called it Polar.

Everyone had gathered at her house to see the kitten and then they decided to finish the go-cart bus they had started the weekend before.

Sarah was holding Polar in her lap. Andy and Megan were fussing over it. The kitten lifted its paws and tapped playfully at their wriggling fingers. They laughed. Barry and Jack were putting the final touches to the braking system on the go-cart bus. Jack had come up with an idea: a simple lever that could be pushed forward to rub on a wheel and bring the cart to a stop. All four wheels had one. Jack called it his special feature, a bit like an air bag.

Barry thought it was a bit too much. It had taken too long. The sun was setting behind a bank of broken cloud and still the bus hadn't

forth in his seat to try to make it go faster. His rocking had little effect. The bus was gaining speed anyway. It rattled and clinked down Ridley Road, carrying six very excited passengers. Their laughter and squeals echoed around the neighbourhood. Barry had firm control of the steering rope and was playfully zigzagging the bus as it gathered speed.

'Not too much,' said Sarah, trying to control her laughter. 'Or we might tip over.'

'Good point,' said Jack. 'We are a little top heavy.'

'We're fine,' said Barry as he pulled the rope to the left.

The feeling of the wind through their hair and the rhythmic bouncing up and down on the seats was thrilling. The vibration was like a tickling machine. They laughed and laughed. Harley's tail was wagging even harder. He sat and lifted his nose to the air, enjoying the smells that rode on the wind. His big ears flapped and his eyes watered. He barked once or twice to show his appreciation of being included in the fun.

If the bus gathered too much speed then Andy and Megan, ever cautious, would pull back gently on their brake levers to keep things under control. They made sure Barry didn't see them.

They were nearly at the bottom of Ridley Road when Sarah suddenly stopped laughing. She had spotted something on the road ahead. She leant forward in her seat, narrowing her eyes.

Jack saw her. 'What's up?' he called.

Sarah strained her eyes. She turned to Jack and, pointing, she said, 'Little orange flags ahead. Another trench!'

Barry froze as soon as he heard the word *trench*. 'Huh?'

There was a strip of orange flags lying on the road's edge, near number twenty-two.

'Go round it, Barry,' said Jack. 'Go out wide, we'll miss it.'

They all hung on. Barry went to steer out wide when there was a loud explosion and a cloud of blue smoke drifted into the sky near the park. The van from the rented house came jerking awkwardly around the corner, virtually blocking Barry's escape route.

'Brakes!' Jack shouted as Barry steered back toward the little orange flags.

Everyone pulled their levers as hard as they could. Andy's tore off in his hand. Harley fell off his seat and landed on his belly. He tried desperately to regain his footing as the bus skidded sideways and then began to spin. He decided to jump off.

The bus rattled and banged louder than ever. It jumped and skidded as the wheels slid across the dirt and stones. Everyone cried out as they spun toward the kerb. With the sound of crunching metal and splitting wood, the bus bumped up over the kerb and cannoned into the rubbish bin outside number twenty-two. The bin fell with a crash to the ground as Andy's seat came away from the cart and he tumbled to the footpath. '*Whoa*!' he shouted.

Sarah slid across her seat into Barry, who bumped up against Jack, who was then sent flying from his seat onto his bum into the gutter.

The friends were in shock. There was a stunned silence before anyone spoke. 'Are you all right, Andy?' Megan called as she ran to the aid of her brother.

Andy was sitting up looking at his elbow. There was blood on it. He hated the sight of blood. 'I'm okay,' he replied. 'Just took some skin off my elbow, that's all.'

Megan took out a handkerchief. It was her father's so it was nice and big. She wrapped it around Andy's elbow. He looked away. The others arrived and helped Andy to his feet. Barry was about to give an account of the skills that he had used to keep such brilliant control of the bus when his attention turned toward the van. It had just lurched to an awkward stop and parked a few metres away from them.

The driver must have seen the children crash and yet he or she had not stopped and offered to help.

Barry scoffed. 'Huh! Nice of them to stop and help,' he said.

'Who was driving it?' Sarah asked.

Brushing himself down, Jack joined the conversation. 'Whoever it was disappeared in a hurry.'

Barry suddenly grabbed Jack's arm. 'Look!' he whispered, motioning toward the van. Jack looked and so did everyone else. The van appeared to be empty.

'Look at what?' asked Megan, louder than Barry thought she should've.

'Shh!' he hissed. 'Behind the van.' He was whispering. 'On the other side. Feet.'

Barry was right. Looking under the van toward the front, the children could see two shiny black shoes. They started to move, as if whoever was wearing them was creeping.

Barry edged away from the group, moving closer to the van. Suddenly a hooded figure wearing a long black coat ran from behind the van. Barry was startled and stepped backwards. He kept his eyes on the running figure. The collar of the coat was raised to hide the face. The face turned to him, a glance. It was so pale! Barry stumbled back toward his friends. He didn't turn to see where he was going. His friends had been startled as well and had grouped themselves closer together. Barry was falling backwards and no matter how hard he swung his arms he simply was not going to regain his balance. He fell into the trench they had tried so hard to avoid in the bus. '*Oomph!*' The driver of the van disappeared down the side of the rented house as Barry disappeared down the trench.

Barry grunted as he stood up as quickly as he could. His head popped up from the trench. He had dirt on his face and brown muddy marks on his shirt. He wasn't concerned about his appearance or any injuries. 'Did you see that? Did you?' he demanded.

Everyone nodded but didn't know what to say.

'I told you there's something weird going on here, but you wouldn't listen. You had to wait until the vampire arrived?' he said.

'No, Barry. No, not again. Come on,' said Sarah, shaking her head. 'Think about what you're saying. Just because someone wears a black coat doesn't mean they're a vampire.'

Jack laughed mockingly. 'You are amazing,

Barry. First we get the gorilla, then the witch and now the vampire.'

'You were scared,' said Barry. 'You jumped back just like me.'

'It was just the way they ran out from behind the van, that was all.'

Barry put his hands on his hips. 'Okay, you explain it to me then. Why did that ... that ... *thing* hide its face? And why did it hide from us in the first place? Come on, explain that to me?'

Jack shook his head. 'All right, I can't, but I'm sure there's a reason.'

'Like what?'

'Shy.'

'Hiding big fangs more like.'

Jack turned away. 'You're crazy. The young girl is probably going to a costume party or something.'

Andy and Megan had hold of the steering rope of the bus and were pulling it up the street.

'We're heading back to Sarah's,' said Andy. 'I need to get something on my elbow.'

'Good idea,' said Barry. 'Don't let fang features in the rented house see that blood.' Barry licked his lips for effect. Andy quickened his step.

Sarah was thinking, trying to come up with an explanation for the actions of the cloaked stranger. Out of the corner of her eye she saw Harley rummaging in the upturned bin. She could only see his tail, and it was wagging furiously as usual. No doubt he had found some tasty morsel to munch on. Barry was wandering cautiously toward him. The bin lay next to the gate of the rented house.

Barry didn't want to be hanging around the house any longer than was absolutely necessary. He called to Harley in a forceful tone. 'Harley, get out of there! Get out!' But Harley wasn't taking any notice. His head was lost in the depths of the bin and his tongue in luscious food scraps.

Barry marched over to him and tugged at his tail in an attempt to drag him out, but Harley dug his back feet in and put his brakes on.

Sarah came over to help. Jack had walked off with Andy and Megan. Sarah tried calling and patting her legs playfully. 'Come on, Harley! Come on, let's go. Come on.'

Barry kept one eye on the house as he pushed and pulled Harley. 'Right! I'm going, Harley. That's it!' he said impatiently. But Harley wasn't silly, he knew Barry wouldn't leave without him.

Sarah suddenly had the idea of standing the bin up again. Barry bent to help her and as they lifted the bin Harley slid out with something in his mouth. He dropped it as Barry and Sarah stood the bin upright.

Harley quickly snatched up his treasure, but not before Sarah and Barry caught a glimpse of it. They both stood open-mouthed. The image would remain printed on their memories of a piece of wrinkly skin covered with strands of grey hair.

'Get that off him!' said Sarah.

'I will if I can,' said Barry.

Harley could sense by their sneaky approach that Barry and Sarah were going to take his treasure away from him. But he wasn't going to give it up. It was nice and chewy. He took off up the road.

Sarah and Barry ran after him, calling him. 'Harley! Harley!' They shouted to the others for help. 'Stop him! Stop Harley! He's got something horrible in his mouth!'

With that, the chase was on. As Harley ran all he could think of was where to bury his find so no one else could have it.

As Sarah and Barry ran all they could think of was, had they really seen what they thought they saw?

Chapter 5

Harley was tearing around at breakneck speed. Dodging, weaving, bounding, jumping. Barry and his friends were chasing him. Harley remembered this game from when he was a puppy. He liked the chasing game. He'd learnt it at home with the family. He would steal something like a slipper, a ball or a nice piece of meat from the table near the barbecue and then everyone would chase him. But they never caught him. They would run and yell and slide and jump but never, ever did they catch him. It was that feeling of success that spurred Harley on to play the chasing game whenever the opportunity arose. They would get cross with him sometimes, but not for long. He'd just look sad, roll on his back and whimper. The pathetic look never failed.

Harley had left the children behind. He was nearly home and was heading for his secret place. He ran to the side of the shed, through a thick bush and under the rusty old car wreck at the far end of the yard.

Jack was running alongside Sarah and had all but given up the chase. He stopped, bent over with hands on knees, trying to catch his breath. 'What has he got in his mouth anyway?' he puffed. 'I didn't get a proper look at it. What's horrible about it?'

The twins were standing next to Jack, waiting on Sarah's reply.

She pretended she couldn't catch her breath enough to tell them. She wasn't sure whether or not she should tell them what she *thought* it was. Barry came to her rescue.

Huffing and puffing, he swallowed and said, 'Dead skin. Did you see the dead skin?' Jack and the twins looked at him blankly, uncertainly. Sarah bowed her head. Barry pulled her into the conversation. 'It's not just me this time, Sarah saw it too. Didn't you, Sarah?'

Sarah shuffled her feet nervously and tossed her head back in search of another big breath. Then she nodded. 'Yes, I did.'

Megan wasn't happy. 'Hold it, hold it. I'm not quite sure what you're saying here.' She tipped her head curiously to one side. 'Did you say dead skin?'

Barry was about to explain but stopped himself. 'You tell them, Sarah. They'll just think I'm nuts.'

Sarah looked over her shoulder, back down toward the rented house. 'That stuff flapping

from Harley's mouth, well he got it out of the bin.'
She paused, and the others hung on her every
word. She took a deep breath. 'It looked very
much like skin with some hair on it, grey hair.'

There were three very shocked faces staring
open-mouthed back at Sarah. If Barry had told
them they wouldn't have given it much thought.
But coming from Sarah it was a different matter.

Jack looked at her and frowned. 'Are you sure,
Sarah?'

Sarah shook her head. 'Well no, of course I'm
not. That's why we wanted to catch Harley so we
could get a closer look.'

Megan's face buckled. 'I feel sick.'

Andy screwed up his face. 'Me too.'

Barry did little to help their stomachs settle.
'The skin was all wrinkly,' he said, wriggling his
fingers. He stopped and stood as if frozen. 'I've
got it!' he said. 'Aliens! That's what it will be.
Aliens that shed skin and can make themselves

look like anyone they want to. I bet they pulled the skin off the old lady and had some left over so they threw it in the bin.'

Megan turned away and groaned.

'What about the vampire, Barry?' asked Jack. There were a few seconds of silence and awkward glances.

'No, it's probably not a vampire. The cloak was to hide its weird appearance, that's all.'

Jack shook his head. 'Let's find Harley,' he said. 'I want to have a proper look at this skin. Where do you think he is, Barry?'

Barry shrugged his shoulders. 'I don't know, in the backyard somewhere.'

Andy turned to Barry. 'Harley wouldn't eat it, would he?'

Barry made repulsive gobbling sounds and nodded his head.

Everyone moaned.

'Come on,' said Jack. 'Let's go find Harley.'

'No need,' said Sarah suddenly, pointing toward Barry's house. 'There he is.'

Harley trotted out of the driveway wagging his tail and looking very happy with himself. He had nothing in his mouth.

'Oh no,' Megan moaned. 'He's eaten it.'

'He's never licking my face again, ever!' said Andy. 'In fact, I don't like him at all anymore.'

Harley bounded up expecting the usual friendly greeting but they all moved away from him as he approached. He thought they were cross with him because he had beaten them at the chasing game. He rolled onto his back and went into pathetic mode. Much to his surprise, they didn't pat him.

Barry looked at Harley's front paws and noticed dirt. 'Look!' he said. 'He hasn't eaten it, he's buried it!'

'It's somewhere in your backyard, Barry,' said Jack. 'Let's go.'

Barry rubbed Harley's belly. 'Come on boy, get up, come on.' He turned to the others. 'He might just lead us to it if we encourage him.'

Harley was suddenly the centre of attention and he loved it. 'Come on, Harley. Let's go home,' Sarah said sweetly. 'Where did you dig boy, hey? Where's the skin? Show us where the skin is.'

'Oh no, no,' moaned Megan. 'Can we not mention the skin, please.'

Jack ran on ahead with Barry and beckoned Harley to follow. Harley bounded after them.

When they arrived at Barry's house and made their way to the backyard, they took one look around and realised how hard their search was going to be. The yard was a mess. There were two old car skeletons as well as a scattering of rusty car parts and motorbike bits. Not only that, but Harley was a compulsive digger and there were mounds of dirt everywhere. Harley had spent some of the day amusing himself in a digging frenzy, so many of the mounds were freshly dug.

'This is hopeless,' said Andy, who wasn't keen on digging for bits of skin. 'We'll never find it in here.'

'Yes, you're probably right,' said Sarah. 'But we can't give up without trying. We might be able to pick the freshest mound.'

So they started examining the mounds but Harley had been too clever for them, they didn't even think to look under the old car wreck by the shed. They dug into a couple of mounds but found only dirty old bones.

They all gave up after a while and sat thoughtfully at the front of Barry's house. The go-cart was parked next to them but no one was interested in it anymore. There was tension within the group, a nervous tension. A feeling of uneasiness was making everyone uncomfortable. After a while Sarah couldn't stand it any longer.

She felt the need to convince herself that what they were thinking was too ridiculous for words.

'It was probably just a piece of plastic or something,' she said, trying to put her mind at ease. 'Maybe even a kid's toy.'

'Yes,' said Megan. 'Maybe, but it would be good to be sure though.'

'And the hair,' said Andy quickly. 'Could be that the person is a hairdresser and needed to toss out some hair from one of the jobs they'd done.'

Jack nodded. 'Yes, of course, that could be it. There simply has to be a logical explanation.' He stood in front of the group. 'Look, I think we should go down and say hello. Just knock on the door and say hello.'

His suggestion wasn't greeted with great enthusiasm. Barry was particularly edgy. He started walking around in a circle. 'No thanks, not me.'

Jack tried to reason with him. 'Barry, can't you

73

tell how crazy this is? You see an old lady you think is a witch, then you think she's got some spell that can make her young again, just before you see the vampire run to the house and Harley pick up some wrinkly skin shed by an alien! It doesn't make sense. You've been watching too many scary movies.'

Barry considered Jack's argument. It did sound a bit ridiculous. He sprung quickly to his own defence. 'You saw how sneaky the thing was when it got out of the van.'

Jack patted Barry on the back. 'We saw someone in a black cape. A very nice black cape.'

'Sarah saw the skin, all wrinkly and hairy!'

'She said she couldn't be sure what she saw.'

Barry folded his arms. 'Well you tell me what you know about this person then. The house has been lived in for a week and no one knows anything. Not even the adults in the street. They have no idea who or what lives there. My mum and dad don't know. Do yours?' Barry looked at each of his friends in turn to gauge their responses. They all shook their heads. He was right. None of the parents knew anything. 'So right then, Jack,' he said forcefully, 'it's up to us. Let's go! Lead the way and we'll knock on their door.'

Jack wasn't sure he wanted to go at that very moment but he felt cornered. All eyes were on him. It was his move. 'Oh, well, right,' he stammered. 'We'll go now, shall we?'

'Might as well,' said Barry quickly before the others could answer. 'No point hanging about.'

The sun had just gone down. It would be dark soon. Andy looked up at the streetlight above them as it flickered to life. 'Maybe we shouldn't disturb them now. They might be eating.'

'Hmm, eating what?' said Barry, rolling his eyes.

Sarah hit him in the arm. 'Stop it, Barry!'

Jack stood up and began walking along the road. The others followed, almost in single file. They looked like a little gaggle of untrained soldiers. They were silent as they walked.

They reached the front of the rented house and stood at the gate. They paused before they moved along the path.

As they approached the open front door of the house, Jack suddenly put his arm out and stopped. He put his finger to his lips. 'Shh!'

They could hear voices. Three, maybe four. One of them sounded like a child, a little child. Curiosity pulled the group closer toward the house. They moved slowly, cautiously.

Just then Harley pushed his way between them and wandered, sniffing, into the garden of the rented house.

'Harley! Get out of there,' Barry hissed.

Harley ignored him.

Barry slapped his leg. 'Harley, get here, now!'

Harley disappeared down the side of the house.

'I'm going to get him,' said Barry quietly.

Sarah grabbed his arm. 'Don't worry about him. He'll come out in a minute.'

Barry looked at Sarah, his face etched with determination. 'I'm going in.'

He turned and took three creeping steps toward the house. He froze on the spot when he heard the sinister sound of deep-throated laughter.

A light clicked on in one of the front windows and filtered out eerily into the passageway. Through the open front door the spies fixed their gaze on a moving shadow.

Barry stared, as did the others. Was the light playing tricks or were they really looking at the moving shadow of a man with a beard and ... and only one leg?

Chapter 6

The children took off. They ran up the street and back to Barry's house. They scurried into the letterbox bush for a meeting. It was getting dark so Barry rushed into his house and brought out his torch. It was a torch he took camping with him and had switches and knobs everywhere with all kinds of emergency lights on it.

He scrambled into the bush with the torch's orange hazard lights flashing. He was flicking switches and turning dials. All he wanted was the ordinary torchlight but he couldn't figure out which switch to use. He managed to turn the blinking orange lights off but then a red light flashed on. Then came the noise, a beeping sound obviously designed to attract attention if he was ever lost in the bush. Barry was frantic in his attempts to silence the torch. He was in a flat panic and suddenly began thumping it on the ground and cursing it under his breath.

Jack snatched the torch away from him and turned off the loud beeping. He handed the torch back to Barry and showed him what to do. 'It's this button here, Barry. The blue one.' He clicked it on. The torch lit up. 'See.'

Barry clicked the blue button on and off a few times. 'I knew that. It was stuck a minute ago.'

Barry was straight onto his alien angle as soon as he'd settled with his torch. 'You can see what I mean now, can't you? If it's not witchcraft then it has to be an alien thing. I mean, changing their form, their voices. They can make themselves look like or sound like anything or anyone. And

'We'll set up some observation points,' said Jack.

'You mean we're gonna spy on them?' said Barry. 'We're not gonna knock on their door and say hello?'

'I just think we need to find out a bit more about them,' he said.

Barry was excited. 'Right, let's do it.' He looked out toward the street. It was very dark now. 'Maybe we should start tomorrow.'

So it was agreed. There was to be an intense observation of the rented house. They discussed how they were going to go about it. After ten minutes of fierce debate a plan was hatched. It was decided that Andy and Megan would be doing regular passes of the house on their rollerblades as they pretended to play in the street. They would create a diversion if anything went wrong. Barry was going to hide in the trench at the front of the house and do some spying with one of Jack's homemade cardboard periscopes. Sarah was going to fly her kite, get it stuck in the tree across the road opposite the house and then climb the tree to get it down. She would stay in the tree and get a clear view of the house and the backyard from the treetop. It was a perfect spying place.

Jack wouldn't say what he was planning for himself. 'I'm not going to tell you. It's a surprise. I'll get it finished tonight and it will be perfect for what we want.'

Barry hated secrets. 'Why won't you tell us what it is?'

'Just in case I don't get it finished.'

'Is it something to do with submarines?'

'I'm not saying, Barry.'

'A torpedo! We can strap it to our bus, roll it toward the house and blow 'em up if they're aliens.'

'No, Barry. Give up, I'm not telling you.'

Barry tried a different approach. 'It's probably weak anyway. Probably won't even work.'

Jack smiled. 'I'm off, I've got work to do. I'll see you tomorrow morning. We'll meet here at eight o'clock.' He crawled out of the bush.

'Is it big, this thing you're making?' Barry called after him. 'Big or small?'

Jack whistled as he walked out across Ridley Road.

Barry put his hands on his hips. 'I might just make something as well. I've got a good idea.'

Jack walked on. The twins were following him.

Barry spoke to Sarah as she walked away. 'Jack can be a toad sometimes, can't he?'

Sarah nodded. 'We all can.'

'What are you going to do now?' asked Barry.

'Go home and play with Polar.'

'Take good care of that cat,' Barry warned. 'Don't let Harley get near him.'

'Sure, Barry. See you tomorrow.'

'Right, see you tomorrow.'

Barry walked along his driveway. He was thinking of Sarah's cat when he suddenly realised that Harley hadn't been at the meeting. In fact, he hadn't seen Harley since he disappeared down the side of the rented house. Barry stopped in his tracks. He panicked. He turned and yelled into the darkness. '*Harley*!'

His friends stopped walking and looked back at Barry. He was running now toward the rented house, the light from his torch flying in all directions. The desperate pitch of his voice and the echo of his footsteps created an eerie atmosphere. The others couldn't help but follow him.

Chapter 7

Barry was in a panic. In just a few seconds he had convinced himself that Harley had fallen victim to the aliens, vampires and witches who lived in the rented house. Images of his beloved Harley having terrible alien things done to him raced through Barry's mind as quickly as his feet pounded the footpath. Who knows what they would be doing to him? Barry was suddenly afraid that he might be finding bits of Harley's skin and fur in the rubbish bin. As his fears deepened and became more horrible, Barry's voice became louder. 'Harley! Harley!' he called.

When Barry finally made it to the rented house he stood and looked down the driveway. He was puffing but managed to keep his torchbeam steady. He saw something black and lumpy by the side fence. It was motionless. He took a few cautious steps forward to see if he could make out what it was. His heart was pounding. It was Harley, he was sure of it.

Barry was about to run down the driveway when Sarah arrived, followed quickly by Jack and the twins. Sarah grabbed Barry. 'What's wrong now?' she asked.

He didn't say anything. He pointed down the driveway with one hand and kept his torchlight focused on the black lump with the other. He swallowed. 'It's Harley. They've done him in.'

'Oh no!' gasped Andy and Megan together. 'Where is he?'

Jack pushed through to the front of the crowd. 'He was here only a few minutes ago. Let me see.'

He took the torch from Barry. He couldn't make out what it was they were looking at. 'You mean that black lumpy thing by the fence?'

Barry nodded. 'I'm going to get him.' He walked away slowly. No one tried to stop him. They stayed, keeping one eye on Barry and the other on the rented house.

Barry wasn't thinking scary thoughts about what might happen to him if the weird neighbours got hold of him, all he could think about was Harley. Harley was his friend, his buddy, his little brother almost. He glanced at the house and suddenly felt anger building inside him. If they had done anything to his Harley then they were going to get it. Jack would bring home one of his father's torpedoes and they *would* strap it onto the go-cart, push it at the house and blow the place up. 'You wait,' Barry mumbled, glaring at the house. 'You just wait.'

Jack was feeling sick in the stomach as he watched Barry sidle nervously down the driveway. He loved Harley as much as the rest of them and he liked Barry as well. He didn't want to think about Barry kneeling and lifting up the floppy body of Harley from the cold ground and carrying him home in the darkness. He didn't want to think of Barry being unhappy. Barry was annoying sometimes, but always fun to have around. So was Harley. They were alike in so many ways, Barry and Harley. Jack too started to feel anger toward the occupants of the rented house. He was thinking of revenge as he watched Barry stop and stand motionless over the black lump.

Everyone held their breath as Barry crouched down slowly.

'I can't look,' said Megan, turning away.

The others stood silent as Barry reached down to scoop up …

'Hey!' Barry cried out suddenly, jumping to his feet. 'It's a rug! A big fluffy old rug!'

Jack shook his head. 'I knew it! I just knew it! Barry is an idiot! He gets us …' He clenched his teeth and didn't finish his sentence. He thrust the torch into Sarah's hand and started marching away. He was in front of Sarah's house when he finally stopped and realised he had better go back to the others and help them find Harley.

'He's probably at home eating beans,' he grumbled. He had taken only one step back toward his friends when he heard a strange sound. It was coming from somewhere in Sarah's front yard. Frowning, he stopped and listened. He heard it again. He squinted as he moved quietly toward the front fence and scanned the yard.

Sarah's yard was a mess of bits and pieces, so

it was hard to see anything. Her father didn't seem to mind what he brought home from his building jobs. Jack couldn't imagine how Sarah could live with it all. Mind you, the things her father collected came in handy at times.

Jack rested his hands on the low fence. He thought he heard two sounds. They were both coming from the same place: to his right, over near the house and next to the side fence. He was going to call out to the others but then thought it best to investigate himself. He didn't want to tell them to come and check it out if it was something silly. Barry would really be able to give him a hard time then.

Jack jumped Sarah's fence and made his way warily through the maze of junk. The sound was clearer now. He was getting closer. He stopped when his path was blocked by an old kitchen cabinet. It was only waist high but he didn't need to climb over it. The sound was coming from behind it so all he had to do was take a quick look. Jack knew what it was but just wanted to check to make sure. He leant over slowly, sneakily, and took a peek.

Jack moved back through the maze to Sarah's fence. He was just in time to greet his friends who had ambled back across the road. They were busily making plans for the Harley search.

Sarah had taken charge. 'You go and see if he's home, Barry. The rest of us will patrol the street and down near the park. He won't be far away.'

Jack was grinning at them. 'What about your kitten, Sarah? When was the last time you saw Polar?'

Sarah's face changed completely. So did Barry's.

'You don't think they've got both Harley and the cat, do you?' he asked.

Jack slowly shook his head.

Barry scratched his ear. His face was a picture

of horror. 'Oh no! I hope Harley hasn't taken Polar somewhere to eat him.' He looked at Sarah. 'I told you Harley was vicious when it came to cats.'

Sarah took a step toward Barry and was about to respond angrily when Jack moved between them. 'There's nothing to worry about,' he said in a calm voice. 'Just follow me.'

He had everyone intrigued as they scrambled over Sarah's fence. They followed him without question. Halfway through the maze Jack turned to them and put a finger to his lips. 'Shhh,' he said.

He stopped at the old cabinet and motioned with his finger for everyone to look behind it. Four curious faces peered over the cabinet. They all smiled. Harley appeared to be fast asleep on an old two-seater lounge. He sensed he was being watched and opened one eye. He didn't jump up to greet them, though. He didn't want to disturb the little white kitten that was fast asleep nestled up against his big hairy belly. Harley grinned at them and gave his tail three little wags. He whined softly as Polar slept.

'It's Jack's secret,' she said. 'He's made a little helicopter.'

It was clear to them now. The small flying machine buzzed ever closer until it flew in circles above their heads. Harley kept barking and the children laughed, including Barry.

Jack walked across the street as he kept a keen eye on his flying machine. He landed it safely on the roof of Barry's father's four-wheel drive. Everyone ran to look.

'That's amazing, Jack,' said Andy. 'When did you make this?'

Jack lifted it down off the car and spun the rotor blades with his fingers. 'Dad and I finished it last night. I would have had it finished sooner but someone skidded the back wheel of their bike into it when I was working on it last week.'

'Who did that?' said Barry innocently.

Jack looked at Barry with raised eyebrows.

Barry suddenly remembered. 'Well *I* didn't know what you were making.'

Sarah looked over Jack's shoulder. 'What are you going to do with it?'

Jack turned the little craft upside down. 'I'm going to do some spying.' He pointed to a thin pen-like attachment on the bottom of the helicopter. 'This is a camera. Dad bought it for me.'

'Oh wow!' Megan couldn't hide her excitement. 'That's amazing! So we're going to get a video of the house?'

'Well, no, not a video. It only takes still pictures, digital pictures. Then I can download them onto the computer.'

'That's great,' said Andy.

'I don't know how clear they'll be, though.'

'It's worth a try,' said Sarah.

'Yeah,' said Barry a little stunned. 'It's worth a try.' He looked down at the remote control. He reached for it. 'So how do you work this thing?'

Jack pulled the remote control from Barry's fingers. 'No way, Barry. You're not getting your hands on this.'

Barry turned his attention back to the helicopter. He spun the blades with his fingers. 'Where did you get all this stuff from anyway?'

'It's actually a couple of model aeroplane kits that my dad and I modified.' Jack frowned studiously. 'You see, we needed a large propeller and what we had to do was —'

'Yep, okay, whatever,' interrupted Barry. He didn't feel like listening to one of Jack's technical lectures. 'Let's just get on with what we're here for.' He picked up the periscope Jack had brought across for him.

There was some discussion about whether they needed to change the plan they had devised the day before. Barry suggested that perhaps the little helicopter could do it all alone. But eventually it was decided they should stick to the original plan. They all wished each other luck and set off to take up their positions: Jack with his little helicopter, Barry in his big boots with his periscope, the twins on their rollerblades and Sarah with her kite.

Sarah struck problems immediately. Her kite wouldn't fly. There wasn't enough wind to lift it. Eventually though, and with some help from Jack, she threw the kite up into the tree, where it got stuck. They were sure the people — or whatever they were — in the rented house hadn't seen them.

Jack set himself up behind Mrs Moroney's small blue car. He could see through the side windows and still remain well hidden. The first thing he noticed was an unsteady periscope wobbling about from within the trench across the street.

Barry couldn't see a thing. All he could make out was fence and long grass. He moved along the trench from one end to the other, trying desperately to find a clear spying spot. All the children could see his periscope as he moved along the trench. From up the tree, Sarah could see all of Barry. She couldn't help but giggle as she watched him in his big boots trudge from one end of the trench to the other. He stumbled and nearly fell twice. All the time he kept the periscope glued to his eyes, just in case something did come into view.

The twins were grinning as well. They watched the periscope as it moved back and forth like a small mechanical toy that was out of control.

Everyone was settling into their positions when they suddenly heard a mournful, wolf-like howl. The spies froze and listened. It came from the rented house and was followed by another howl … then another … and another.

Barry dropped his periscope in fright. Something was happening and the spies were in the perfect place to witness it. They were lucky … or were they?

Chapter 9

Barry panicked. His periscope lay uselessly at his feet, his back was pressed against the wall of the trench and his eyes were open wide in fright. The howling didn't stop. It was loud and then soft. Long and then short.

Barry began to think the worst. What if the aliens came out of the house and found him in the trench? There would be no escape! He was trapped. Maybe that's what the trench was: a human trap. The creatures were howling to tell each other that they had caught something. Yes, that was it. They would be coming soon, coming to get him. How could he be so stupid? Why didn't he think of it before? He had to get out.

He reached up and began to scramble to freedom. His desperate fingers clawed at the soft earth and his chubby legs kicked for grip. His enormous boots were no help at all. Grunting and groaning he heaved himself up, his clothes covered with mud. He kicked, pulled, clawed, heaved, groaned. He was out! He stood huffing and puffing. Suddenly he heard the buzzing sound of the tiny helicopter. He turned to face it.

Jack was fumbling furiously with his controls. Something was wrong. The helicopter wasn't responding properly. It had dipped and was flying too low. He was trying desperately to get it to climb, but it wouldn't.

The helicopter was heading straight for Barry. It looked as though it was on target and going to hit him right between the eyes. Barry cried out and ducked at the last moment. The helicopter missed him but Barry lost his balance and fell backwards into the trench. 'Aaagghhh!'

Sarah had been watching Barry. She wanted to race over and help him out but uncertainty as to the origin of the howling made her hesitate. She stayed in the tree and hoped Barry's head would once again appear above the top of the trench. After a moment, it did.

Barry scrambled back out of the trench. He moved awkwardly away from it toward the footpath. He kept his head down as he wasn't keen on falling victim to another vicious dive by the miniature helicopter.

Jack was feverishly twisting and turning the controls. The buzz of the little helicopter was uneven; it would sputter then rev, sputter then rev. Its flying pattern had become unpredictable. One instant it would rise sharply toward the sky and the next it would be plummeting like a wounded bird toward the ground. Up and down, up and down it went. All the time it was heading toward the rented house.

The howling continued and could be heard clearly above the sound of the little craft. Barry ran as fast as his enormous boots would allow. He headed for home and the sanctuary of the meeting bush. As he ran he kept looking over his shoulder to check whether he was being pursued. He stumbled numerous times but managed to keep his feet. He looked around for his friends to check what their reaction had been, not that that would stop him. What they decided to do was entirely up to them and if the howling-beast-alien-vampire-skin-shedding things ate them then that was their fault.

Sarah didn't move from her lookout. The howling was frightening but she chose to stay where she was. Barry was out of his trench and she figured being up the tree was one of the best places to watch the action. She had a perfect view of everything and could still make an escape if she needed to. She told herself that the things in the rented house would not want to come across the street after her and show themselves. They would, she thought, be more secretive and sinister in their attacks on humans.

The twins were so pleased to be on their rollerblades. They were cruising along the footpath directly in front of the rented house when the first chilling howl escaped into Ridley Road. They had not hesitated. As soon as they heard the sound they exchanged terrified glances and took off up the street. Their escape was swift. They waited near the letterbox, calling to Barry to get a move on. 'Hurry up, Barry. They've seen us. They know what we're up to. They're coming to get us.'

Jack wasn't prone to panic attacks. He was

normally well composed in a crisis but the plight of his little helicopter was of great concern to him. He didn't want to see it smash into a thousand pieces in a terrible crash. It was one of the best things he had ever made. He and his dad were proud of it. He found himself being drawn from his hiding spot behind Mrs Moroney's car as he tried desperately to save the little machine. He stepped out onto the road as the helicopter sputtered toward the front of the rented house. He stood in the middle of the road flicking the controls and fidgeting madly. His head and body mirrored the dodging, twisting, diving and soaring movements of the little craft. Then ... *smash!*

The helicopter went straight through the front window of the rented house.

Jack was snap frozen with shock. He stood, almost breathless, in the middle of Ridley Road. He could hear his little helicopter still buzzing about like a mad mechanical blowfly and the howling inside the house changed dramatically to screaming.

Sarah decided it was time to get out of the tree. She abandoned her kite and scrambled down through the branches like a possum in a panic. She scratched her right arm on the way down but didn't stop to check the injury. She jumped from the tree and hit the ground running. She ran toward Jack. She knew she had to snap him out of his frozen state. Her cries were loud and desperate. 'Jack! Jack! Let's get out of here, come on!'

Jack turned to look at Sarah. His mouth hung open but he couldn't speak. He turned back and looked down at the remote control. He wriggled a switch. They could hear the helicopter buzz on. He looked at Sarah and shrugged his shoulders pathetically.

Sarah snatched the controls from him. She

threw them to the ground. 'Forget it, Jack. Just leave it.' She grabbed his arm and pulled him into a reluctant jog.

'But ... but ...'

The sound of smashing glass and terrified screams had stopped Barry and the twins in their tracks. They had no idea what had happened to the helicopter or why Jack was standing in the middle of the road staring at the rented house. Barry immediately assumed that one of the things had come out of the house and shown itself. Funnily enough, the twins had similar thoughts.

When they saw Jack and Sarah suddenly running up the street toward them, the next obvious assumption they made was that the things were not only out of the house but they were now pursuing their friends.

Sarah was tugging hard on Jack's arm to keep him moving. He was stunned and it wasn't until he tripped on a bump in the road and tumbled like a parachutist making a very bad landing that he suddenly snapped out of his silent state. Sarah stopped and tried to help him up.

He pulled his arm sharply from her grasp. 'Let go! I'm going back.'

Sarah's disbelief was obvious. 'What?' she puffed. 'What for? Are you nuts?'

'The helicopter. Dad and I built it together. I'm going back to get it.' He stood up and started moving away from Sarah.

She took two paces toward him. 'We're not coming to get you if you're captured.'

Jack ignored her. He ran down Ridley Road and didn't stop until he got to the front fence of number twenty-two. He paused and stood looking at the house. The screaming had stopped and so had the buzzing of the helicopter. He was puffing and his right hand had a bloody graze on it from when he had fallen on the road. He ignored the stinging. He had to get his helicopter. He stared at the broken window, the sharp, jagged needles of glass; the pieces that had fallen into the garden. The star-like spattering across the concrete path that ran beneath the window. The thin net curtains were tangled in the broken glass like a spider web tangled in a rocky place. From the road Jack tried to see inside. He craned his neck and moved through the gate into the front yard.

The sound of Barry's enormous boots pounding the road's surface made Sarah turn around. Barry was clumping toward her. 'What's he doing? What is that nut doing?'

Sarah shook her head. 'I don't know. He thinks he can go and get his helicopter.'

Barry put his head in his hands. 'Oh no, I don't believe it. I always thought he was a clever kid, you know. But now, he's a goner.'

Barry's comments brought no response from

the others. The twins heard him and didn't know what to say. Sarah, for once, agreed with Barry. But what were they to do? Stand there and watch or go down to help Jack and end up becoming victims themselves. Barry spoke to his friends. 'I don't think I'd like the feeling of having my skin peeled off.'

They all stood, their stomachs churning, and watched Jack move cautiously closer to the front door of the house. Together they crossed to the other side of Ridley Road so that they could see the front door clearly.

Jack was taking his time. His head was constantly turning, checking to his left, to his right and behind him. His muscles were tight, his breathing faster than usual, his hands shaking. He stood at the door, straightened his hair with his fingers and tugged at his shirt and pants. He was plucking up the courage to knock. The tension he was feeling was being relayed directly to his friends. Andy and Megan had their hands clasped in front of their faces as if they were praying. Sarah had taken a strand of her long hair and was sucking on it. Barry was biting his fingernails.

Jack lifted his shaking fist to knock on the door. Suddenly it was flung open. Jack screamed like he'd never screamed before. Fear had glued his feet to the ground. He stood, straight and stiff, and screamed a long gut-wrenching scream. He thought he was going to pee himself. His knees went wobbly.

The others could see that the door had been flung open but couldn't see what was standing in front of Jack. Without thinking they ran down Ridley Road and in an instant were also screaming. There, at the door, standing in the shadowy passageway stood a wolf-like beast on two legs with its front paws on its hips.

With the scream forcing all of the air from his

lungs, Jack heaved for a breath as he turned to run. The wolf-like beast was after him and his friends didn't hang about to see what would happen next. Friend or not, Jack was on his own.

'Aaaagh! No! Let go of me! *Noooooooo!*'

Chapter 10

Jack had fallen by the fence just as he was trying to scramble over it and make his escape from the beast. He was on the ground, face down, when the creature bent over him and clawed at his clothing. Like a soldier in training, Jack tried to pull himself along the ground using his elbows but it was no good, the beast had him. He kicked furiously and called out at the top of his voice, 'Help! Help! Somebody help me!'

The beast grabbed him firmly by the shoulders, turned him on his back and sat on him. Jack looked at the beast's fangs and the glass-like eyes that seemed to stare right through his very being. Then it lifted its enormous paws to its head. Jack closed his eyes. He didn't want to see the claws come slashing toward him. The thought of his skin being torn and peeled from him like apple skin in a shredder was too much to bear. 'Noooooo!' he screamed.

The others heard Jack's cries. Then there was silence. It was the silence that halted them in their tracks. It was worse than the screaming. The end had come.

The twins were the first to dive into the letterbox bush, followed closely by Sarah. Barry was a few steps behind them. His enormous boots had slowed him down considerably. The four crouched closely together in the bush. No one said anything. There was just a lot of huffing and puffing, sighing and groaning.

Megan wanted to cry. She liked Jack a lot. He shouldn't have been eaten or had his skin peeled off, or whatever it was the beast things did to him. She should've done something. How could she have just left him to die? She looked round at the others. How could they live with themselves, knowing they hadn't lifted a finger to help Jack? There was no going back now, they had made their selfish decision and they would have to live with it. The thoughts of guilt and betrayal fell like an avalanche on Megan's small shoulders. They rounded as she slumped into a gentle sob.

Andy felt like Megan. He rested his hand on her back.

Barry bowed his head. He couldn't look at anybody. He swallowed and stared down at his fingers, writhing like wrestling worms in his lap. He closed his eyes tight then opened them again. He blinked quickly over and over and over again.

Sarah was ashamed of herself. She wasn't looking forward to Jack's funeral. At least now though, she thought, these things that lived in the rented house would be exposed. Jack hadn't died in vain. He was a hero really. She repeated that thought to herself. Jack had died a hero. It didn't make her feel any better. It wouldn't bring him back.

Barry looked up when he heard Harley barking. He listened intently. The barking was coming from the street. Someone had let Harley out of the house! Before Barry could push his way from the bush he heard Harley run past them and into the backyard, barking all the way.

The others looked at Barry questioningly. They scrambled onto their knees and on all fours peered out through the scratchy branches of the bush. They heard voices. One was a boy's voice, croaky but familiar. The other was a young woman's. There was giggling.

Sarah recognised the giggling. Jack? She stood up and pushed her head through the thin branches at the very top of the bush. She looked like a real-life jack-in-the-box.

Barry tugged at her legs. 'What is it? Who's out there?'

Megan stopped sobbing and waited quietly for Sarah's reply.

'It's Jack,' said Sarah, dumbfounded. 'He's alive.'

Barry tugged at her leg again. 'But is it *really* Jack, or is it one of those things that has taken his skin and is *pretending* to be Jack?'

Sarah bobbed down and began to push her way out of the bush. 'Barry, look for yourself,' she said, 'I think you'll get the idea.'

Barry stood up and peered out the top of the bush. He saw Jack strolling up the road toward him. He was laughing. He was carrying his helicopter, or what was left of it. He was walking with a young woman with long shiny dark hair. Barry could only see her hair because the rest of her was covered in fur. She was dressed in a wolf suit and carrying the wolf's head under her arm.

The bush dwellers crawled out from their hiding place. Jack stopped when he saw them coming. 'Here they are,' he said to the young woman. 'My friends, the ones who left me at the mercy of the cruel beasts and beings of the rented house.'

The girl tossed her head back and laughed.

Jack waited for the others to come closer. Barry was still unsure and stayed at the back of the group.

Jack introduced his companion. 'This is Kelly. She's an actress. You may know her better as the vampire in the television advertisement for Blood Curdling Bubblegum.'

They all looked at each other. Jack continued.

'You may also know her as the pirate in the television advertisement for Treasure Chest chocolates.' The friends responded to this information with casual nods and murmurs of recognition and realisation. Jack didn't stop there.

'She also does voices for radio. She can do any kind of voice you want, even a baby's voice.' Jack turned to Kelly. 'Do one for us, Kelly. Please?'

Kelly blushed a little. 'Oh okay.' The expression on her face changed and she proceeded to do a baby voice, complete with dribbles and farting noises. Kelly laughed when she finished. The others laughed along with her. They were amused but also fascinated and relieved.

Barry still needed to straighten things out. There were a few points he wasn't clear on. 'What about the skin stuff Harley was chewing on?' he asked.

Kelly smiled. 'It's amazing stuff, isn't it? The make-up crews can make me look like anything they want. It's a bit like clay really. You can mould it to make masks. I use it mainly to add a few wrinkles and warts and things. I've even used it to make myself look old.'

'She was a witch the other week,' Jack added quickly. 'A broomstick company wanted to do some posters.'

Megan looked down at the wolf's head. 'And the wolf?'

'A car alarm,' said Kelly, lifting the head. 'It's going to be called a Howling Wolf car alarm. I was just getting some howling practice in when Jack's helicopter smashed through the window and frightened the life out of me.'

'Is this what you always do for a living?' asked Andy.

Kelly sighed. 'Well, I don't mind it, but I want to be a real actress, in Hollywood.' She looked up dreamily to the sky. 'I want to be in movies and play some real parts. I want to be able to drive around in limousines.' She looked across at her old van. 'Not that old thing I've got just now. I

130

don't want to spend the rest of my life being witches, wolves and the like.' She turned back to her little audience. 'You know what I mean, don't you?'

They nodded. They understood perfectly.

'Anyway,' she said matter-of-factly, 'what about helping me clean up the mess the helicopter made? I can show you some of my favourite advertisements I've made over the past two years. I've got them all on video. You might even remember them.'

There was no argument, no hesitation. The rented house sounded like the place to be!

Chapter 11

Over the next few weeks the people of Ridley Road saw Kelly dressed as a goblin, Batman, Santa Claus and even a giant knife for a margarine advertisement. And in the evenings after school the friends spent a lot of time at the rented house. She told them about her experiences as a young, struggling actress. She told them many secrets about television and radio: how people fly, how they fall off tall buildings and how they disappear. The spies told Kelly how frightened they had been of her.

'I knew it would've looked a bit weird,' she

said. 'I raced around because I didn't want anyone to see me. I was a bit embarrassed.'

Barry grinned. 'You can't keep secrets from us, you know.'

Kelly smiled. 'Yes, I know that now. You are a pretty good bunch of spies.'

'Not spies,' said Jack. 'Just interested neighbours.'

Sarah looked at Kelly. 'No, you're right,' she said apologetically. 'We are spies.'

Kelly waved a dismissive hand. 'Don't apologise. I should've introduced myself, and besides, you can never be too careful.'

The people of Ridley Road took great interest in Kelly's career in the weeks that followed. They watched for her appearances on television and listened on their radios for her voices, howls and screams.

Kelly had been living in Ridley Road for only six weeks when her van exploded for the last smiling. She could see they were happy for her. 'I'm leaving this weekend.'

Joining hands, they all jumped about in a dance of celebration. At that moment, the fire brigade arrived which prompted more dancing.

Kelly drove away from Ridley Road on a quiet Sunday evening. She had a new car and had promised the Ridley Road children she would write and let them know how she was going and also to let them know when the movie was to be released. They stood waving to her as she drove down the road toward the park, around the corner and out of sight.

Barry finished waving and turned to his friends. The rented house was behind him. He chose not to look at it. 'She was fun to have around, wasn't she? I think she'll be a star.'

Megan nodded in agreement. 'I think she will too.'

Jack looked at the rented house. It seemed so small, so insignificant, so lonely. 'I wonder who our next neighbour will be?' he said.

'Or *what* our next neighbour will be,' added Barry, smirking.

His friends turned on him. They howled him down and playfully slapped him until he turned and ran from them with Harley barking at his heels.

Phil Cummings' understanding of the way the youngest readers see the world and talk about it has made him one of Australia's most successful picture book writers. *Angel* was his first novel and a runaway success and won the CROW focus book award. In 1998 Phil was awarded the prestigious Carclew Fellowship at the Adelaide Festival of Arts Literary Awards. Phil divides his time between writing and teaching and lives in the Adelaide Hills with his wife Sue and their two children.